Start-Off Stories

THE GOOD WITCH

A Charles Perrault Tale Retold

By Mary Lewis Wang

Illustrated by Melodye Rosales

Prepared under the direction of Robert Hillerich, Ph.D.

CHILDRENS PRESS®

CHICAGO

Library of Congress Cataloging-in-Publication Data

Wang, Mary Lewis.
The good witch / by Mary Lewis Wang.
p. cm. — (Start-off stories)
Summary: A good witch rewards a helpful sister and a selfish sister in kind.
ISBN 0-516-02368-3
[1. Fairy tales. 2. Folklore—France.]
I. Title. II. Series.
PZ8.W196Go 1989 89-34415
398.2—dc20 CIP
[E] AC

Printed in the United States of America.
1 2 3 4 5 6 7 8 9 10 R 98 97 96 95 94 93 92 91 90 89

Pearl helped at home.
Frances did not.

Every day Pearl went to get water.
Frances did not.

One day when
Pearl went out,
she met an
old woman.

"May I have some water?"
asked the old woman.

"Why, yes," said Pearl.
"Let me help you."
She did not know this was
a good witch.

"You are so good,"
said the good witch.
"I will do something for you.
When you get home,
you will know what it is."

"Here is the water," said Pearl. As she spoke, flowers and jewels came out of her mouth!

“What is this?” said Frances.
Pearl told Frances about
the old woman.

Frances said, “I want flowers.
I want jewels, too.
I will get more water.”

The witch was there, but now
she was not an old woman.
Frances did not know who
she was.

"May I have some water?"
asked the good witch.
"I did not get this water
for you," said Frances.
"Find some water over there.
You will get no help from me."

The good witch said,
"You say little that is good.
But I will do something for you.
When you get home,
you will know what it is."

"Here is the water,"
said Frances.

As she spoke,
snakes and toads
came out of her mouth.

"Look what you did to me!"
said Frances.

"Help, help!" said Pearl.

A prince saw
the flowers.
He saw
the jewels.

So he came
to find Pearl.

From then on, Pearl was as happy as she was good.

From then on,
Frances said
very little.

WORD LIST

a
about
an
and
are
as
at
but
came
day
did
do
every
find
flowers
for
Frances
from
get
good
happy
have
he
help
helped
her
here
home
I
is
it
jewels
know
let
little
look
may
me
met
more
mouth
no
not
now
of
old
on
one
out
over
Pearl
prince
said
saw
say
she
snakes
so
some
something
spoke
that
the
then
there
this
to
toads
told
too
very
want
was
water
went
what
when
who
why
will
witch
woman
yes
you

ABOUT THE AUTHOR

Mary Lewis Wang is the author of three other Start-Off Stories: *The Lion and the Mouse*, *The Frog Prince*, and *The Ant and the Dove*. She also has edited many books for both children and adults as an editor with McGraw-Hill, Golden Books (Western Publishing Co.), and John Wiley & Sons. A native New Yorker, she is now a resident of St. Louis, Missouri. She and her husband are the parents of three grown children.

ABOUT THE ARTIST

Melodye Rosales has been an illustrator for ten years. After finishing the University of Illinois at Urbana, Ms. Rosales went on to attend The School of The Art Institute and Columbia College, both in Chicago. The Good Witch was particularly special because it is her first fairy tale. As advisors for this book, Melodye consulted experts in the field of imagination: her own two children.